THE
SIXTH-GRADE
MUTANTS
MEET THE
SLIME

THE
SIXTH-GRADE
MUTANTS
MEET THE
SLIME

LAURA E. WILLIAMS

A YEARLING BOOK

Published by
Bantam Doubleday Dell Books for Young Readers
a division of
Bantam Doubleday Dell Publishing Group, Inc.
1540 Broadway
New York, New York 10036

The trademarks Yearling® and Dell® are registered in the U.S. Patent and Trademark Office and in other countries.

ISBN: 0-440-41317-6

Printed in the United States of America
July 1997
10 9 8 7 6 5 4 3 2
OPM

*With special thanks to Tim Wengertsman,
Ashley Kearney, Charissa Y. Kearney, and Amanda
Wilke—my young critiquers*

This book is dedicated to my son, Chad Kiernan. He's not a mutant yet, but he sure wishes he were, especially when it's time to clean his room, or do his homework, or set the table. . . .

THE
SIXTH-GRADE
MUTANTS
MEET THE
SLIME

CHAPTER 1

"You're a slimeball!" I screamed. Then I slammed the door in my little brother's face. He was such a pain. I don't think I was ever that bratty when I was seven. Of course, that was a long time ago—now I'm eleven.

There's a lot more about me I should tell you, besides being eleven, I mean. But if I tell you all of it at once you'll probably close the book in disgust. Basically, you just won't believe me.

So, let me tell you everything as it happened. But first, I want you to know that I've changed all the names in the book to fake ones. Even the name of our school is fake. Why? To protect me and my friends, of course.

Oh, and one more thing. Everything in here is true. I swear it.

*   *   *

It started last fall during the first week of school. Mr. Verde, our science teacher, was called down to the office at the beginning of class. After glaring at us and warning us all to behave, he rushed out of the room.

Big Jim, practically the biggest kid in the whole school, stood in front of the room and puffed out his chest. Then he stalked back and forth in front of the glass cabinets that held all the chemicals. "Guess who I am," he said.

Everyone booed him.

"You look like a stuffed sausage," Cecilia Mason said. Cee is my best friend. We sat next to each other at the high black-topped tables. We laughed at her joke.

Big Jim ignored Cee. He stopped in front of Mr. Verde's lab table and picked up an empty glass beaker. Then he poured a bunch of different-colored liquids into it from the vials sitting on the table.

"I don't think you should do that," Iona Smith said from the back of the room.

"Scared?" Big Jim taunted. He kept pouring. The mixture in the beaker started to froth and bubble.

Cee and I looked at each other nervously. It was one thing to imitate Mr. Verde, but it was another thing to mess with his chemicals.

"What's that stink?" I asked, wrinkling my nose.

Cee held her nose and shook her head, her long, tight, beaded braids swinging against her face.

"I think you'd better quit it," Rick Agent said. Rick

sits behind me and Cee, and we both have a crush on him. He has dark curly hair and gorgeous blue eyes.

"Yeah," said Sue Duffy, agreeing with Rick. She has a crush on him too. I have to admit that Cee and I are a little jealous of her because Rick always punches her in the arm. Once, he pulled one of Cee's braids, and he borrowed my science book overnight, but he never punches us.

Anyway, then Big Jim said, "I'll just add this last bit." He took a small vial from one of the glass cabinets behind the desk. The cabinets were usually locked. Mr. Verde must have forgotten to lock them when he rushed out of the room.

Slowly, Big Jim poured the bright yellow liquid into the beaker. Now the concoction really bubbled, kind of like Mom's soup when she forgets about it on the stove. It also gave off a greenish light that glowed upward on Big Jim's face as he bent over it. He looked like a green monster. I shivered, even though I knew he was only Big Jim, class clown.

Suddenly green smoke billowed up, filling the room with a thick fog and a horrible stench. We all groaned and fanned the air in front of our faces. But it was no use.

I began to feel faint.

I looked over at Cee. She suddenly closed her eyes and slumped over the table.

CHAPTER 2

"Wake up, Cee." I tugged on one of her braids but she didn't move.

"Open the windows! Open the windows!" Po Po Sidon shouted.

I could barely see through the thick green soup. Kids bashed into tables and chairs as they tried to get to the windows to open them. Chris Squires tripped and fell over one of the chairs. He howled with pain, holding his wrist.

I started to cough. Others around me were coughing, too. I felt really dizzy. The room started to twirl out of control, and I had to put my head down next to Cee's and close my eyes to stop the spinning.

Finally someone got a window up.

Just at that moment, the door slammed open. I

4

lifted my head and opened my eyes in time to see Mr. Verde barge in.

"What's going on in here?" he bellowed.

The open classroom door let in a crosscurrent. Very quickly, the green haze blew out the window. Right away I felt better.

I bent over Cee and gently shook her shoulder. "Cee, wake up."

Her dark brown eyes flickered open.

"Are you okay?" I asked.

She looked around the room as if she didn't know where she was; then she nodded. The beads in her hair rattled. "That was some experiment," she mumbled.

I looked over and saw Big Jim sitting at his lab table, trying to look innocent. I squinted. Yup, he still had a bit of a green glow to him.

Mr. Verde stood in front of the room, his skinny arms crossed over his checkered shirt. "Now, I expect someone to tell me what just happened."

No one said anything.

I looked around the room.

Iona looked a bit pale. Rick grinned at me and my heart skipped a beat. I could feel myself blushing and I quickly turned back to the front of the room.

Mr. Verde stared at me. "Ms. Price, perhaps you would be so kind as to tell me who the culprit is in this fiasco."

I shrugged. No way was I going to be a snitch.

"What's the matter, Ms. Price, cat got your tongue?"

I hated it when he called me by my last name. My name is Jennifer, but everyone calls me JP—everyone, that is, except for Mr. Verde.

"No, sir, I still have my tongue. See?" I said; then I stuck it out to show him. I guess I shouldn't have done that. I knew it even before it was all the way out, but I just couldn't help myself. Sometimes I'm like that. I do stuff before I think it through.

Everyone laughed, and Mr. Verde's face turned bright red. He grabbed the bunch of passes off his desk and started to scribble furiously. He ripped off the top one and held it out to me with a stiff arm.

"Here you go, young lady. Down to the office."

I started to get up.

"Take your books with you, Ms. Price. You won't be returning today."

I grabbed my backpack. Cee looked up at me and grinned. I knew she wished she could leave Mr. Verde's class, too. Everyone probably wished it.

I took the pass and walked out of the room, trying not to imagine Rick staring after me. He probably thought I was a real jerk. In sixth grade, sticking your tongue out is not cool. It's something my little brother would do.

I groaned. Oh, great, here I was in middle school, acting like my dumb brother.

Thinking about my brother reminded me of my parents. I winced. They would not be too pleased about what I'd done. They probably wouldn't let me come to the Saturday Swimathon. Other than the Halloween dance, which was weeks and weeks away, the Swimathon was the only thing to look forward to.

My shoulders sagged. I was supposed to be on Rick's relay team. I couldn't miss that! I just couldn't. Maybe if I told my parents how mean Mr. Verde was and how he tortured us every day—

"Help me!"

I whirled around. Big Jim staggered out of the classroom, clutching his throat. He fell to one knee.

"Heeeelp!" he wailed. Suddenly his eyes rolled back and he collapsed on the linoleum.

CHAPTER 3

My heart jumped up to my tonsils, and I nearly choked on it as I ran toward Big Jim. It was that greenish glow. I just knew it. It was killing him.

I crouched down next to him and tried to roll him over. Remember, this is almost the biggest guy in the school. And I'm not exactly huge.

I was sweating by the time I'd flipped him onto his back. He flopped over like a fish out of water. Better make that a whale out of water.

"Big Jim, are you okay? Speak to me!" I cried. I heard the panic squeezing my voice.

Suddenly his eyes flew open. He grinned. "Gotcha!" he crowed.

I stood up. "You creep," I said, glaring at him as he lumbered to his feet. "That was really slimy of you."

Big Jim didn't even look sorry. "Yeah, I know," he said.

I turned on my heel and stalked away, sizzling with anger. Listening to his laugh as I walked all the way down the hall didn't help any.

When I got to the office I sat on *the bench*. The bench is reserved for kids who get sent out of the classroom for misbehaving. I had never had to sit on it before.

Sandy Lukas walked in and I shrank against the wall, hoping she wouldn't notice me. I was in luck. She looked right through me and didn't even bother giving me one of her snotty smirks. She gave the secretary a folded piece of paper and then left.

I relaxed. Sandy is not my favorite person, even though she's the most popular girl in school. Everyone wants to be her friend. But if she was going to notice you, you wanted it to be when you were starring in a basketball game or wearing the coolest outfit at the dance. Not when you were sitting on the bench like a dummy.

Tipping my head back, I wondered when the secretary would call me into the principal's office. I kind of hoped she wouldn't notice me. Maybe they'd forget about me altogether and I wouldn't have to go to math next period. Math is my worst subject.

But after a while I got bored, and I felt kind of

stupid sitting there all by myself. Finally I walked up to the counter.

"Excuse me," I said.

Mrs. Rant, the secretary, looked up at me. "Yes, JP?"

"Uh, Mr. Verde sent me down to the office." I slid the pass across the counter.

"You, JP? Whatever did you do?" She took the pass and read it. She clucked her tongue like a chicken. "I can't believe you would do such a thing."

"It was kind of an accident," I explained, brushing my bangs out of my eyes.

Then she frowned. "JP, this pass says you were sent down here at eleven-forty-five."

I shrugged. "That's right."

She tapped her watch. "It's now twelve-twenty. Class is almost over. Where have you been all this time?"

I stared at her with my mouth open. "What do you mean where have I been? I've been sitting right over there." I pointed to the bench.

Mrs. Rant's face turned red. "Now listen, young lady. I have been in this office the entire time, and you certainly were not sitting on that bench."

"But I was," I protested. "I saw Sandy come in and give you a note. And the janitor came by with those flowers for you. Oh, and Mr. Strikes popped his head out about fifteen minutes ago and asked you to make a golf appointment for him."

10

Now her face looked really red. Almost crimson. She leaned over the counter and stabbed the wooden top with a pointed finger. "I did not see you, so don't lie to me. You were not there, young lady, unless of course you're invisible." She practically spat out those last words.

I dodged the spit. But then it hit me—no, not the spit . . . the awful truth.

CHAPTER 4

I was invisible!

Yeah, right. That was why Mrs. Rant stared right into my eyes as if she wanted to melt me down into a heap of scrap metal.

But why hadn't she seen me before? Did she need new glasses? My heart started to slow down. Of course, that was it. Mrs. Rant was going blind.

Then I remembered Sandy and the way she'd looked *right through me*. Come to think of it, I realized neither the janitor nor the principal had noticed me either. Could everyone at Kiernan Middle School be going blind?

That was the stupidest thought I'd ever had. I groaned.

"What's the matter?" Mrs. Rant asked.

"Uh, it's nothing. I just have a headache," I said. It

was true. My heard pounded as if fifty basketballs were bouncing around in it.

Suddenly Mrs. Rant looked concerned. "Why don't you go sit down? I'll tell Mr. Strikes you're out here."

I nodded, hoping she would forget about the time problem with my pass. Obviously, she just hadn't seen me sitting there. No one had seen me sitting there. Not because I was invisible, but because—

"JP, Mr. Strikes will see you now."

I walked into the principal's office and sat down on the bright orange chair in front of the desk. He pressed his fingers together like a steeple over his rounded stomach.

"What's this all about . . ." He looked at the pass. "JP?"

I explained everything, conveniently leaving out Big Jim's part in it, although I was tempted to rat on him after the way he'd scared me in the hall.

Mr. Strikes nodded through my whole story. "So, where did you go before you came here?"

I sighed. "Nowhere. Honest. I came right here from Mr. Verde's room."

Mr. Strikes frowned. "I didn't see you out there when I asked Mrs. Rant to—uh, type up a letter for me. I'm almost sure I would have noticed you." He tapped a pencil eraser against the desk.

"Maybe you looked out when I was bending over

13

to tie my shoe," I suggested. "You wouldn't have been able to see me with the counter in the way."

He thought for a moment with pursed lips; then he nodded, his frown smoothing away. "That's probably what happened. Now that I think of it, I do remember seeing a backpack on the bench. Yes, I'm sure of it." He brightened as though he'd just invented chewing gum or something.

I tried to smile as I tucked my feet under my chair. It wouldn't do for the principal to see that I was wearing shoes without any laces.

He sent me on to math class without giving me a detention or anything. Maybe he was just relieved because he remembered seeing my backpack. Maybe he didn't want me telling anyone that he'd made a golf appointment for Thursday morning when he should be in school. Whatever the reason, I was glad my parents wouldn't have to hear about my time on the bench. And now they couldn't keep me from the Swimathon in two days!

The rest of my classes passed slowly. I couldn't concentrate on anything, and of course that was the day every single teacher had to call on me at least twice. I think teachers have radar for that kind of thing.

After school I crawled onto the bus. My head still throbbed. I sat on the front seat because I knew everyone would fill up the back of the bus first.

Chances were, no one would sit next to me, which was fine because I wanted to be left alone.

And I was left alone.

No one even looked at me.

Not even Cee said hi as she walked past. She must have figured I felt yucko because I sat in the front. She didn't want to bother me. That's what's so great about best friends—they really know how you're feeling and they don't bug you.

The bus driver closed the doors.

"Wait!" It was Cee, yelling from the back of the bus. "JP's not here yet."

Chills shivered up my back. The flesh on the backs of my arms prickled. Slowly I stood up in the aisle and faced the back of the bus.

CHAPTER 5

"Where's JP?" Cee called again.

I raised my hand and waved it wildly. Didn't they see me? Was I truly invisible or were they playing a joke on me?

I opened my mouth to say something, but Big Jim stood up. "She's probably still in the office," he said. "Maybe she got a detention. Or maybe she got expelled!"

Cee looked worried. She stared out the window and I knew she was looking for me.

The bus driver called, "Okay, kids, sit down. Time to go. JP will have to walk."

I stood next to the driver as she pulled away from the curb. No way would she have started driving with me standing there. Not even for a joke to make me *think* I was invisible.

16

That proved it.

I was invisible.

I flopped back onto my seat, hoping I'd stay invisible for the rest of the ride. If I suddenly appeared there'd be a lot of questions, and I didn't think I had any answers for them.

As the bus bounced along, I breathed in through my nose and out through my mouth, trying not to pass out from fear. What had happened to me? My heart stomped around in my chest and refused to calm down.

Luckily, Big Jim got off at the same stop I did, so I just slipped out before he got to the door. I waited for him on the sidewalk. When I was sure he didn't see me, I tripped him.

I know, I shouldn't have done it. But he didn't get hurt, and the surprised look on his face was worth it. Also, the kids on the bus razzed him as the bus pulled away.

Big Jim looked around for what he'd tripped on. Then he shrugged and headed home.

I headed home, too. Fast.

At home, I went straight into the bathroom and locked myself in.

I looked in the mirror.

Somehow I had been hoping all this really had been some huge, elaborate joke.

But no.

17

There I was, plain as day. Or rather, there I *wasn't*, plain as day.

No way could I deny the fact now. I was invisible.

I was a freak.

A mutant.

My tongue stuck to the roof of my mouth. I touched my face. At least I could still *feel* me. But now Rick Agent would never even look at me twice. Heck, he wouldn't even be able to see me. I didn't have a chance with him. Not that I minded so much if he ended up liking Cee better than me, but the thought of Sue Duffy getting him made me burn.

If only I weren't invisible, then I'd still have a chance with Rick. I wished I were visible.

Suddenly my form took shape in the mirror. There I was, a real, solid person. My hair was still blond and in need of a trim, my eyes were still green, my nose still too perky.

How did I do it?

I frowned. My image frowned back.

I racked my brain, going back over the day, trying to figure out how I had turned myself invisible and visible again.

I wished I were invisible again so I could test it.

Voilà! (I learned that word in French class—it means "ta-daaaa!")

There I wasn't again.

I was gone.

Invisible.

I wished myself visible and *Voilà!* I was back.

I couldn't help grinning. It was a relief to know I actually had control over this power.

Great, now I could be invisible when it was time to set the table, but pop up when Mom needed someone to lick the frosting off the spatula. Maybe this freaky power would come in handy.

My mind started whirling with the possibilities. I was thinking of all the tricks I could play on my slimy little brother. Or on Big Jim. He deserved some practical jokes. I couldn't help giggling when I imagined what his expression would be if I dropped a toad on his desk. Maybe even a pickled frog from one of Mr. Verde's jars!

This was great. Suddenly I didn't mind being a freaky mutant. As long as I could control the power.

Watching myself carefully, I turned invisible again. I could feel my lips grinning, even though I couldn't see them.

Someone banged on the door.

CHAPTER 6

Immediately my heart raced and sweat slicked my palms.

Was I visible or invisible?

Should I be visible or invisible? I looked in the mirror. Invisible.

Did I really want my family to know about this mutant power I had? I decided it might unglue them, so I'd keep it a secret. At least for now.

I wished myself visible again, and I looked in the mirror. Good, there I was.

I rushed to unlock the door. I should have taken my time, though. It was only my bratty brother, Brian.

"Jeez, you take long enough in here," he said as he slid by me into the bathroom. "Nothing's going to help."

I narrowed my eyes at him and put my hands on

my hips. "Nothing's going to help what?" I should have known better than to ask. I think Brian took lessons from Big Jim.

"Your face!" he said, laughing as if he'd made some great joke.

"Ha, ha," I said. I left him in the bathroom. He was probably going to mix mouthwash with shampoo in the drinking cup (which is why the water in the bathroom always tastes soapy) and pretend to be a mad scientist or something.

That's when it dawned on me. My power had started right after choking on that green haze in Mr. Verde's room.

A tingle raced down my spine. A lot of kids had breathed that stuff. Could they become invisible too?

Just then the phone rang.

I ran to answer it, hoping it was Cee. I really needed to talk to my best friend.

"JP, you're home." It was Cee.

"Hi, yeah, I missed the bus so I walked."

"Did you get in trouble in the office?"

"Not really."

"Did Strikes ban you from the Swimathon?" Cee asked.

"No. I didn't even get a detention." I tugged on my bangs. How should I tell her the big news? I wondered. Finally I just blurted out, "Hey, listen, I have to tell you something, but promise not to get upset."

21

"Ricky asked you to the Halloween dance!" she cried. "I knew it. I knew he liked you better." I heard a tiny bit of envy in her voice. "But I'm really happy for you, JP," she added. That's why she's my best friend.

"No, Cee, it's nothing like that," I said soothingly. "It's about what happened in Mr. Verde's class."

"You should have seen him."

Confused, I shook my head. "Seen who?"

"Mr. Verde—isn't that who we're talking about?"

"Yeah, but—"

Cee interrupted me. She does that a lot. "He went wild when he found out someone had used that little vial of yellow liquid from the glass cabinet."

I raised my eyebrows. "How wild?"

I could tell Cee was shaking her head because her beads rattled against the receiver. "Really crazy. I thought he was going to throw a chair out the window. Even Big Jim looked scared."

"He was just afraid Mr. Verde would find out he was the one who did it."

"Probably. Anyway, after his fit, he sank into his chair and didn't move for the rest of the period. We had a spitball fight and he didn't even care."

"I wonder what was in that vial?" Even as I said the words, I knew it had to have something to do with my new power. But what on earth could weird Mr.

Verde, with his awful checkered shirts, have to do with it?

"Who knows?" Cee giggled. "Maybe it was something to make his hair grow back. Anyway, he did manage to give us some homework."

"It figures," I said as I jotted down the assignment Cee read to me.

"Now, what were you going to tell me?" she asked.

Of course Brian chose that moment to stand in front of me, waiting for the phone. I glared at him. "I can't talk now. I'll tell you tomorrow."

"Righto," she said. She always says that.

We hung up and I handed the phone to my brother. Tomorrow I'd not only tell Cee about my power, I'd *show* her.

CHAPTER 7

The next day on the bus, I didn't get a chance to talk to Cee. Big Jim sat behind us and wouldn't stop blabbering over our shoulders. Besides, Cee was kind of quiet, which isn't at all like her, believe me.

When we got to school, I didn't meet up with Cee again until science class.

Mr. Verde glared at me when I came into class, but he didn't say anything. I went to sit beside Cee.

Before I could sit down, Iona walked by our table. "Did you get the homework assignment?" she asked me.

I nodded. "Hey," I said, tipping my head to one side to study her. "Have you grown?" She probably thought I was making fun of her size. She's the shortest person in the whole school.

Iona blushed. "Uh, I don't think so, why?"

I pointed to her feet. "Your jeans must have shrunk then. Look how short they are." The hems were up above her ankles.

Iona looked down. Her face turned as white as— well, not as white as chalk because the teachers here always use yellow chalk—but she turned really white.

Without another word, she hustled to her table in the back of the room. I sat down and glanced at Cee, but she didn't even look up.

"Okay, class, quiet down," Mr. Verde said, clapping his hands. "Today it's back to business as usual."

"Lucky us," I whispered to Cee.

She just nodded and didn't even look at me or say "Righto" or anything. I examined my arm to make sure I hadn't wished myself invisible by accident. But there I was, as visible as the shiny bald spot on Mr. Verde's head.

It isn't like Cee to ignore one of my sarcastic comments. Usually she comes back with something even more sarcastic. I wondered what was bugging her.

"First, I'd like everyone to turn in their homework." Mr. Verde started around the room to collect the papers.

I dug my homework out of my backpack and smoothed it on the table. My papers always got wrinkled for some reason.

Mr. Verde walked over to our table. He took my

homework and raised his eyebrows. "Perhaps you should iron your paper next time," he said to me.

The class laughed and my face burned. Some teachers just love making fools of us. I hate that.

Then he reached for Cee's homework. At the last moment he gasped and jerked back his hand.

Cee's homework is usually superneat and un-wrinkled. I think maybe she *does* iron her papers. But this time . . .

I stared in shock as Mr. Verde pointed to her limp piece of paper. Very carefully he then picked up the sheet of paper with two lumpy fingers. He held Cee's homework by the only dry corner.

"What is this soggy mess?" he asked, his nose wrin-kling up, looking a lot like my homework paper.

I glanced over at Cee. Her dark eyes blazed with fury and embarrassment as she stared at the table.

"Ms. Mason, is this your homework?"

Cee nodded stiffly.

"Why is it wet?"

I grabbed her hand to show some sympathy. After all, what are best friends for? But I kind of ended up making a scene and embarrassing Cee even more.

"Yuk!" I yelped. I pulled my hand away from hers. "Your hands are all wet. There's a puddle on the table!"

All the other kids craned their necks, trying to get a better view of the wet table.

Mr. Verde took a hasty step back and inspected the puddle from afar. "Now, what could that be?" Just the way he said it I knew the next thing out of his mouth wouldn't be very nice. "Either you spilled some water, or you've been crying up a storm."

He looked around the room and grinned a horrible grin. "Could it be," he continued, "that your crush didn't ask you to the Halloween dance?"

I gasped. No one laughed at his sorry joke.

There are a couple of teachers in the school who say some pretty mean things, but none of them dare use boyfriends or girlfriends in their insults.

That's going too far.

Cee jumped to her feet and ran out of the room. Being her best friend, I knew the only thing to do was go after her.

I found her in the girls' room. She had shut herself up in a stall and I heard her sniffling back her tears.

"Come on out, Cee," I urged. "Mr. Verde's a jerk."

The door clicked open and she sagged out of the stall. Her shoulders drooped and from the damp patches I saw on her clothes, I guessed she'd been crying quite a bit too.

"What's going on?" I asked. "Why did you cry all over your homework?"

"I didn't!" Cee wailed.

I put my arm around her shoulders, trying to calm her. "Did you spill something on it?"

She shook her head.

"Then what?" I asked. I have to admit I was getting a little annoyed.

She held out her hands. "Look!" she cried.

I looked, and I couldn't believe what I saw.

CHAPTER 8

I took a step back so I wouldn't get my shoes wet. "Cee, what—what happened to you?"

She waved her hands around and fountains of water poured from the tips of her fingers. In a matter of seconds, the whole bathroom floor looked like a giant puddle.

She shook her head. "I don't know, JP. It started last night after my shower. When I was drying off I wondered why I wasn't getting dry and why the towel was getting wetter and wetter."

"Can you turn those things off?" I asked, hoping the water all over the floor wouldn't ruin my new sneakers.

"Sometimes." Cee closed her eyes and screwed her face into a knot.

Slowly the water pouring from her fingertips started

to lessen. Pretty soon only the pinkie on her left hand dripped like a leaky faucet.

"Wow," I said. "That's pretty neat."

Cee looked at me in amazement. "Neat? I'm a freak. A weirdo. Now Rick will never go out with me."

"Yeah, but that's only 'cause *I'm* around," I said with a grin.

Cee gave me a watery grin back. "You really think this thing"—she fluttered her fingers—"is—is neat?"

I nodded. "But you definitely have to learn to control it."

Cee giggled. "No kidding. This morning my mother thought I wet my bed. I told her not to worry, I just spilled a glass of water. She was too relieved to yell at me for drinking in bed."

I turned to the mirror and pretended to fuss with my hair. "Can you control it?"

Cee joined me at the mirror. "I'm working on it. Sometimes one of my fingers drips and I can't get it to stop. But it's a lot better now than it was last night."

She turned toward me. "JP? Where are you? JP!"

I heard the panic in her voice and almost laughed out loud. I tiptoed over to the stall and slammed the door. Cee screamed.

Quickly I reappeared. "Stop yelling," I said. "I'm right here."

Cee whipped around and stared at me with her mouth open.

"Someone's going to think there's a murder going on in here," I added, a stupid grin plastered on my face.

Cee kept staring.

I walked up to her and waved my hand in front of her face. "Hellooooo?"

She blinked. "How—How did you do that?"

"You mean this?" I promptly disappeared. Before Cee had a chance to shriek again, I reappeared. I nodded toward her fingers. "You're leaking."

She looked at her hands and frowned. All her fingers were now dripping. Closing her eyes, she held her hands up and tightened them up like claws. Finally they turned off, even the pinkie on her left hand.

"What's wrong with us?" she moaned, opening her eyes.

I sighed. "I figure it has something to do with Big Jim's experiment yesterday. All that green stuff we breathed in has turned us into mutants or something."

Cee grimaced. "I'd rather not be called a mutant. That sounds like something that would live in the sewers."

"Well, freaks then. Abnormalities. Unclassifieds." I didn't seem to be cheering Cee up at all. "Anyway," I continued, "we are what we've become and there's nothing we can do about it."

"How long do you think these powers will last?"

I shrugged. "Beats me."

Cee twisted one of her many braids. "Do you think we should tell anyone?"

"What, so they can put us in a medical institution and study us under a microscope for the rest of our lives? Or better yet, my brother would probably put me in a circus and charge admission."

Cee chuckled. "That does sound like something Brian would do. But shouldn't we tell our parents?"

"I don't think that's a good idea. Just think how they'll feel to have mutants—uh, I mean, abnormalities—for daughters. It would stress them out."

Cee agreed. "Well, at least we have each other."

"Yup," I said. I put my arms around Cee and hugged her, even though she was a bit damp. She hugged me back.

We sloshed through the water toward the door.

Suddenly Cee grabbed my arm. I was so startled I lost my breath for a moment.

In a low whisper, Cee said, "Maybe we're not the only—uh—mutants."

CHAPTER 9

"I don't know," I said, shaking my head.

"It would be kind of cool to find out if there are any more mutants like us out there. Maybe there's a flying kid, or one with X-ray vision." Cee sighed. "Why couldn't I have gotten something like X-ray vision? Something useful." She shook her damp fingers. "What use will ten waterspouts ever be?"

I shrugged. What was I supposed to say? "Uh, you could water the lawn for your parents," I suggested.

Cee rolled her eyes. "Oh, great, a human hose."

I tried to stifle my giggle, but it escaped.

Cee smiled weakly. "I guess it's a little funny," she admitted. "But just a little. You can call me Hose Girl—the Mutant Kid."

"Hey, I thought you didn't want to be called a

33

mutant kid," I said, my hand on the bathroom door handle.

Cee shrugged sheepishly. "Well, I just don't want other people calling me a mutant. It's okay if I call myself that, or if you call me that 'cause you're one too."

Just then someone banged on the door.

I pulled my hand away with a jerk and tried to slow my racing heart.

Cee and I looked at each other. Had the person on the other side of the door heard our secrets?

Slowly I opened the door.

Mr. Verde stood there with fists on hips. "Are you ladies planning on ever coming back to class?" His voice dripped with sarcasm.

We scooted out and closed the door behind us. What would he say if he saw all that water on the floor?

"We were just coming now," I said. "Cee was pretty upset."

Mr. Verde sniffed. "If such little things upset you, Ms. Mason, you'll never make it when you get to high school."

When he turned around, we rolled our eyes at each other. Teachers are always saying dumb stuff like that. If you don't do your homework . . . If you don't pay attention in class . . . If you don't stop throwing food . . . As if we were really going to act like that when we got to high school. Besides, that's a few years off, anyway.

When we got back into class, Big Jim made a face at us, but I could tell it was just to make Cee feel better. Rick didn't even look up. We both sighed and sat down at the table we shared.

Everyone was working quietly on a lab project.

I raised my hand. When Mr. Verde ignored me, I said out loud, "Excuse me, but we don't have the lab assignment."

Mr. Verde slowly looked up. I could tell he was fuming. He was probably still mad at me for sticking my tongue out at him the day before, and then for running after Cee.

Mr. Verde stared at me, and I stared back. Then I blinked my eyes, sure I was seeing things.

But no, Mr. Verde looked a definite hue of green. He kind of looked like Big Jim right after the experiment the day before.

Maybe he was sick. You know, "feeling green," as my mom always says when I don't feel well enough to go to school.

Oh, gross. I hoped he wasn't going to throw up in front of us, the way Brian once did at the dinner table last summer.

I nudged Cee in the ribs and whispered without moving my lips, "Does he look kind of green to you?"

Cee looked at Mr. Verde, who still glared at me.

She nodded. "Especially around the eyes," she whispered back.

Mr. Verde suddenly turned his back to the class and took a deep breath. His shoulders trembled. Then he pivoted again.

"Look," I said. "The green is gone." Now he was back to his usual pale color.

"I wonder what's up with that?" Cee said.

Suddenly Mr. Verde was standing right next to our table, glaring down at us both. He handed us the lab sheet. Cee and I got right to work.

When the bell rang for class to end, we quickly cleaned up and ran to our next class. It wasn't until after school that we realized we actually had to go back to see Mr. Verde.

"I can't believe you forgot to ask him for tonight's homework," Cee wailed as we headed down to the band room for after-school practice. We had a fall concert in a couple of weeks.

I stopped walking. "*I* forgot? What about you?"

"Now we have to go see him again."

I groaned. Going after school to see a teacher you like is bad enough. But going to see Mr. Verde seemed like the kind of torture a parent would think up.

"We'd better hurry up so we won't be late for rehearsal."

Quickly we turned around and went upstairs to the

science wing of the building. Our classroom door stood open.

"Mr. Verde?" Cee called.

He didn't answer.

"Look outside and see if his car is still here," I suggested as I inspected the glass cabinets. They were locked. I peered through the glass, looking for any more vials of yellow liquid, but there weren't any.

"Yup, his car's still here," Cee called from the big windows.

I shrugged. "Maybe he's down in the teachers' lounge, or in the office. We can check on our way to band."

On the way out of the room, I grabbed the door handle. Immediately I jerked my hand away and almost screamed.

CHAPTER 10

I stared in horror at the gross green slime covering my hand.

The slime hung from my fingers in long strands, and when I shook my hand, trying to get it off, it just jiggled around. Some of it even flew up and wrapped around my wrist.

"Get it off!" I cried. "Cee, do something!"

Cee stood there as if made of stone, her eyes opened almost as wide as her mouth. Finally she shook off her horror and jumped into action. Pointing her index finger at my hand, she squirted water all over it.

Almost instantly the slime melted away. Next Cee washed off the door handle.

It was a good thing no teachers or custodians came by to see the mess we'd made.

We hurried down the hall. "What was that yucky stuff?" I asked, rubbing my fingers together. They still felt a bit slimy.

Cee shook her head. "I don't know. Maybe some gross experiment the eighth-graders are doing. One of the kids probably thought it would be funny to leave that slimy door handle for Mr. Verde."

"I didn't think it was funny."

Cee giggled. "But you have to admit, seeing Mr. Verde scream with all that slime on his hand would have been hilarious."

I scowled at her. "Yeah, but he *didn't* have it on his hand. *I* did. You didn't have to touch the stuff. It was totally gross."

"Righto," she said, patting me on the back. "It wasn't funny at all." But I could still hear the laughter in her voice.

"Did I hear someone say 'gross'?"

We whirled around. Big Jim had sneaked up on us.

"You really shouldn't talk about yourselves like that," he continued, his body jiggling with laughter.

"We weren't talking about ourselves," Cee said sweetly.

"We were talking about you," I finished.

Big Jim laughed outright. One good thing about him (maybe the only good thing?) is that even though he loves to dish out jokes and pranks, he can take them, too.

We all ended up laughing.

"Are you two going to band rehearsal?" he asked.

I checked my watch. "Yup, we're on our way."

"I have to get my trumpet out of my locker," Big Jim said.

"Well, you'd better hurry," I said. "We're all going to be late."

"Not me," Big Jim said. And in a flash he was gone. And I do mean *flash* and *gone*!

CHAPTER 11

Cee and I stared at each other.

"D-Did you s-see that?" I finally managed to sputter.

Cee lifted her eyebrows in doubt. "See what?"

"You mean you didn't see anything?"

"I saw Big Jim here a minute ago."

I nodded. "So did I. But where did he go?"

"He said he was going to his locker for his trumpet."

"But did you actually *see* him go?"

"What are you two blubbering about?" Big Jim demanded right behind us.

Cee screeched.

"How—How did you sneak up behind us?" I demanded. Then I saw the trumpet case in his hands. "And how did you get that out of your locker so fast?"

Big Jim shrugged. "I just ran. Fast."

41

I could see a wicked grin tugging at his lips. I narrowed my eyes at him. "You're playing a joke on us, right? You had your trumpet hidden and then you . . ." It sounded like a lame plan even to my own ears. *But how had he done it?* He couldn't have, unless he had super speed like Superman or something.

"Oh no," I groaned. I finally realized the truth. "The science experiment. It got you, too, didn't it?"

Cee turned to me, her eyes wide. "You mean his mutant power is speed?"

I nodded.

Big Jim looked disappointed that we had figured out his trick. Suddenly he looked surprised. "Hey, wait a minute!" he exclaimed. "What do you mean *got you, too?*"

Now it was our turn to smirk.

Cee flipped her braids over her shoulder. "You mean you think you're the only one with special powers?" With a quick grin at me, she pointed her pinkie at Big Jim and gave him a shot of water right in the face.

Big Jim sputtered and wiped the water away with his shirtsleeve. "How did you do that?"

"You mean this?" Cee sprayed him again.

"Okay, okay," Big Jim protested. "I get it." He turned to me. "And you, too?"

As an answer, I simply disappeared. It was great to see the shocked expression on his face.

"That is so great!" he exclaimed. "I could do tons of practical jokes on people with that power!"

Cee sighed. "You two have neat mutant powers. All I can do is this." She squirted a thin spray of water into the air.

"You could be a fountain in the park," Big Jim suggested.

"Great," said Cee glumly. "Now I'm not Hose Girl. I'm Fountain Girl."

Big Jim and I looked at each other and shrugged. Cee's power did seem kind of useless. But we weren't going to tell her that.

Just then, something behind Big Jim caught my eye. It was Iona walking down the hall carrying her flute case. Something about her looked different. Strange. Weird.

CHAPTER 12

"Hi, Iona," Cee said. "Going to practice?"

Iona smiled. "Yes, I just had to get my flute." She looked at the floor. "What's all this water doing here?"

The three of us mutants quickly glanced at each other.

"JP told the funniest joke," Big Jim said with a grin. "I laughed so hard I peed in my pants."

Cee turned to him. "That is so totally disgusting. I can't even believe you said that."

Meanwhile, I kept staring at Iona. What was it about her that looked really weird? I checked out the hem of her jeans, remembering how short they had been in science class.

I gasped.

Iona saw where I was staring. She looked down at

her feet. Her jeans were now so long they were all bunched up around her sneakers.

"Either you changed your pants or you shrank about five inches," I blurted out.

Okay, so maybe I shouldn't have been so direct, but how did I know she was going to burst into tears?

Immediately I put my arm around her. "I'm sorry," I said.

Cee patted Iona on her back. "Don't cry, Iona. JP has a big mouth."

"Hey," I said.

Cee gave me a look, and I shut up. I could argue about my big mouth later. Right now Iona was upset.

I looked at Big Jim. His face was turning red. I guess he didn't know how to handle a crying female. Guys are so hopeless.

"Why are you crying?" Cee asked.

Iona sniffled and pulled a tissue out of her pocket and rubbed her nose. She shook her head. "It's nothing. Nothing at all."

Cee and I looked at each other. Sure, Iona was blubbering away for nothing. Not!

"Come on, Iona, you can tell us. We're your friends," I said. "It'll make you feel better if you talk about it."

Iona pushed some of her red curls out of her eyes. She took a deep breath. "Okay, I'll tell you," she said in a rush. "I have to tell someone or I'll go crazy. Maybe I'm already crazy." She pointed down to her feet. "Watch."

CHAPTER 13

We all stared in amazement as Iona grew. And grew and grew and grew. I mean *tall*. Pretty soon she was all hunched over so she wouldn't hit her head on the ceiling.

Then, as quick as a lightning bug, she was back to her normal size. Well, almost normal.

"I think you have to shrink a little more," I said, pointing to the hem of her jeans. Her socks were still showing.

Carefully Iona adjusted her height so that her pants were the perfect length. "That's one of the problems," she said. "Sometimes I grow or shrink without even knowing it. Last night, one of my arms got longer than the other when I reached for the brussels sprouts on the other side of the dinner table. Luckily nobody noticed."

Cee wrinkled her nose. "Why would you want to reach for brussels sprouts?"

Before Iona could answer, Big Jim said, "I could be the star of the basketball team with that kind of power." He grinned. "Want to trade?"

Iona's red eyebrows shot up. "Trade? What are you talking about?"

Now we all grinned. All together we squirted water, disappeared, and raced around in eye-blurring circles.

When we'd finished our little show, Iona clapped her hands. "This is perfect!" she cried. "Now I'm not the only freak!"

"Mutant," I corrected her. "We prefer to be called mutants, not freaks."

"Yeah," said Big Jim. "*Freaks* sounds so . . . so freaky."

"We could have a secret club," I suggested. "For mutants only."

"Mutant kids," Big Jim said.

"How about Mutant Kids, Incorporated?" Iona said.

"What's with the *Incorporated*?" Cee asked.

Iona shrugged. "My dad's company's name has *incorporated* at the end of it. Makes it sound more important, I think."

Big Jim rubbed his hands together. "I like it. I like it. Mutant Kids, Incorporated. What will we do in our club?"

"We can just hang out and be mutants," I said. "What else do mutants do?"

"I'll tell you what this mutant did today," Iona said, pointing her thumb at herself. She lowered her voice. "I heard the strangest thing a little while ago. I heard these voices coming through the heating ducts. So I stretched up to listen. It was the two janitors talking. They were talking about some equipment missing from the gym. Big equipment, like parts of bleachers and stuff."

"Why didn't they just report it?" Cee asked.

"That's what I was thinking," Iona said. "But then one of them said there was this strange green slime stuff all around where the missing things used to be. He said he even thought he saw a slimy green thing. He doesn't want to tell anyone because he's afraid he'll lose his job. People will think he's crazy."

Cee and I stared at each other.

"Slimy green stuff?" I managed to choke out.

Iona nodded. "That's all I heard. I had to shrink down when I heard someone coming."

"Those guys must be crazy," Big Jim said with a laugh. "Who ever heard of a bleacher-eating green slime?"

"Wait till you hear what just happened to us," Cee said. "We—"

"Shouldn't you all be at band practice!" a voice demanded.

CHAPTER 14

We all kind of shrieked and yelped. We hadn't heard anyone sneaking up on us. We looked up to find Mr. Verde standing there, glaring.

"Oh, Mr. Verde," Cee gushed, placing a hand over her heart as though to slow it down.

"We were looking for you earlier to get our science homework for over the weekend," I said.

Mr. Verde pursed his lips. "As a matter of fact, Ms. Price, I did not assign any work over the weekend on account of the Swimathon tomorrow." He said *Swimathon* with so much distaste, I thought for sure he'd choke on the word. Plus, I was shocked he hadn't given any homework. He even gave homework on the first day of school!

"That's great," Cee said. "Thanks, Mr. Verde."

Mr. Verde's lips twitched, but it didn't look much like a smile to me.

"By the way," he said as he slowly moved toward the door of his classroom. "How are you children feeling?"

We all kind of looked at each other. What a weird question to ask!

"Feel great," Big Jim said. He thumped himself on the chest. "Never felt better."

Mr. Verde looked at the rest of us through slitted eyes. "Nothing out of the ordinary or—"

"Cecilia!" someone interrupted.

My heart jumped. Only one person I knew called Cee by her full name.

Sure enough, Cee's dad strode down the hall toward us.

"Cecilia, where have you been? I left work early to pick you up, but you weren't waiting where you were supposed to be."

"Daaad," Cee moaned. "I said to pick me up at *four*-thirty, not three-thirty. I have band rehearsal today. Remember?"

Suddenly Mr. Mason's face cleared. He rapped his knuckles on his forehead. "Oh, brother! I got the times mixed up."

"Again," added Cee.

With a smile he held his right hand out to our

science teacher. "I'm Cee's father, in case you hadn't figured that out. Craig Mason."

"I'm Mr. Verde," said Mr. Verde, shaking hands. "You have a wonderfully bright daughter here."

I really wanted to throw up when he said that. Teachers always say that to parents; then they step all over the kids in class when the parents aren't around.

"And her homework is really neat, too. Isn't it, Mr. Verde?" I said. I just couldn't help myself.

"Why, yes, now that you mention it, Cee does lovely work."

Oooooo, he was smooth. Didn't even trip over his words. I hated to do it, but I had to give him credit for that one.

Cee's dad sucked up all the compliments. Parents love that stuff. I thought his teeth would crack, he smiled so hard.

"I must be off," said Mr. Verde. He went into his classroom and grabbed his briefcase, then carefully locked the door behind him. He waved curtly as he marched away.

Mr. Mason opened and closed his right hand a few times, looking at it. "That's strange," he said.

"What is, Dad?"

Mr. Mason shook his head. "It's nothing much, just that your science teacher has really slimy hands."

CHAPTER 15

Cee grabbed my arm. I have to tell you that she has quite a grip when she wants to use it.

"Ow!" I said, pulling out of her clawlike grasp.

She didn't even apologize. "You know what this means, don't you?"

Mr. Mason shook his head. "What does it mean?"

"Oh, nothing, Dad," she said sweetly. It was obvious to all of us she didn't want to tell her dad. "You'll pick me up after practice?"

Her father looked at her doubtfully. "Okay, kiddo, but get on down to the band room." He checked his watch. "You're a little late already."

"Righto, Dad."

"Bye, Mr. Mason," the rest of us called as he walked away.

As soon as he was around the corner, Cee's tongue practically tripped over itself to say, "Don't you guys get it?"

Big Jim burped out the word, "Nope."

Iona glared at him. "You're disgusting."

He grinned.

"Come on, Cee," I said. "What are you talking about?"

"Tell us as we go to band. Mr. S. is going to have a fit if we walk in too late," said Iona, leading the way.

As we hurried to practice, Cee breathlessly told us her theory. "There's been a slime sighting at the school. We found slime on the door handle of the science room. Mr. Verde's hands were slimy. . . . Maybe *he's* the slime!"

That stopped us all dead in our tracks.

I opened my mouth. "But—"

At that second, Rick Agent appeared out of nowhere. "Come on, you guys," he said. "Mr. S. has us out hunting you down. Hurry up."

"We're coming," I said, smiling at him.

He actually smiled back!

Cee elbowed me in the ribs. "We'll meet at my house tonight," she whispered. "We have to figure out this slime business."

We all agreed. Then we eagerly chased after Rick to the band room. At least Cee and I were eager about it.

*　*　*

For dinner that night we had spinach casserole. I know that sounds gross, but it's really very good. In fact, it's one of my favorite meals. But that night, I could barely eat any of it.

"What's the matter, honey?" my mom asked. "You usually wolf down two servings of this."

I picked up a lumpy green mass with my fork and looked at it. It just looked too much like the stuff on the door handle for me to eat it. "I guess I'm not very hungry tonight, Mom."

"She had a ton of cookies after school," Brian blabbed.

I glared at him. "I only had four," I corrected him. "That's not a ton."

"You did not," Brian said. "You had—"

"That's enough," Dad interrupted. "No bickering at the dinner table."

Mom looked at me. "Honey, I need you to pick Brian up at school tomorrow after the Saturday gym program."

"But I can't," I wailed. "I have the Swimathon all day."

"I can stay after gym for the arts and crafts program," Brian piped up.

For once I was grateful to him.

"Fine. You stay after, and JP will pick you up when it's over at two-thirty."

After dinner I said, "I'm going over to Cee's house for a little while. Okay?"

"Be home in an hour," Mom said as I hurried out of the house.

Outside it was dark. I wished it were still summer with long hours of sunlight.

I peered around, but I didn't see anything suspicious. No slimy green blobs, thank goodness.

I did feel a chill down my back, though. It was as though someone were watching me, creeping along behind, waiting to pounce.

I whirled around, my heart pounding.

Nothing.

No one there.

Then I had an idea. I wished myself invisible.

Looking down at my arm, I saw that it'd worked. Great. Now, even if the blob was out there, it wouldn't be able to see me.

Though I felt a bit safer, I still jogged quickly toward Cee's house. When I passed Mrs. Crossely out walking her dog, I whistled.

The dog yipped and barked, sensing me even though I was invisible. Mrs. Crossely looked around nervously and hurried back into her house.

I know, that was pretty mean. Poor Mrs. Crossely probably thought the boogeyman was out to get her.

But now that I think back on that night, I might have saved her life by scaring her back inside.

Just before I got to Cee's block, I stopped. I must have seen something out of the corner of my eye.

Even though I knew no one could see me, I was still scared. Slowly I turned and looked behind me.

The wind rattled through the trees. It was dark and hard to see. But there—there under the dim street-lamp, I saw it.

CHAPTER 16

The green blob started jiggling toward me.

I swallowed my scream and ran as fast as I could all the way to Cee's house and burst into the kitchen. Cee and her mom and dad still sat at the table, eating dinner. They looked up at me, startled.

"How did the door blow open?" Mr. Mason asked, getting up to shut it.

Then I remembered that I was still invisible. My heart thumped away, and I heaved deep breaths. I couldn't believe they didn't hear me. Actually, Cee did look around the room with narrowed eyes.

"Can I be excused?" she asked.

"May I," her mother corrected, the way she always does.

"May I?"

Mrs. Mason nodded. Cee jumped up and put her dishes in the sink. She hurried out of the kitchen. I followed, trying to walk in step with her so that her parents wouldn't hear an extra set of footsteps.

In the living room, Cee whispered, "JP, is that you?"

I tapped her on the shoulder.

She yelped.

"Are you okay, honey?" her father called from the kitchen.

Cee stifled a giggle. "I'm fine," she called back. Then she walked over to the front door and knocked on it. "I'll get it," she yelled.

When she opened the door, I made myself visible.

"Hi, JP," she said, grinning. But when she saw my expression, the grin slid off her face. "What's wrong?"

"Come outside," I said, tugging on her arm.

We stood out on the front step. I peered into the night, but I didn't see any green blob. Had I imagined it?

Cee tugged on my arm. "Come on, JP. Tell me what's going on."

"All right," I said in a hoarse whisper. "On the way over here I saw a green blob. Maybe it knows about our mutant powers and it's out to get us."

Just then Iona walked up the driveway. I told her about the blob I'd seen.

"We have to go hunt it down," Iona said.

"What? Are you crazy?" I cried. "If the thing can slime bleachers, it can slime us, no problem."

"But how will we ever know if it was out there if we don't investigate?" Iona countered.

Cee nodded bravely. "You're right. But let's stay close together."

I gave in with a sigh. What choice did I have?

Slowly and cautiously we all headed down the steps to the sidewalk. Except for the wind, the night was unusually quiet.

Carefully we made our way down the street, jumping at every squeak and scratching sound. I reached out and grabbed Cee's and Iona's hands. We held on to each other as if our lives depended on it.

We'd only gone past two houses when I heard a soft squishy sound under my sneaker. Afraid that someone had recently walked their dog there, I stopped and looked at the bottom of my shoe.

"Gross!" I exclaimed.

Cee bent down to look at the barely worn treads of my brand-new sneakers. "The slime's been here!"

I tried to wipe the clingy strands off on the grass, but they stuck like wet bread dough.

Iona pointed at the ground. "Look! There's more!"

Shoulder to shoulder, we started walking backward.

"Hey," I whispered, afraid to break the silence of

the street and draw the slime's attention, wherever it was lurking. "Didn't there used to be a mailbox here?"

Cee stopped edging backward. "What happened to it?" She looked around. "And where's Mr. Sullivan's car? He always parks it right here."

"Maybe he went out?" Iona's voice wobbled.

"He's over ninety years old. He never goes anywhere at night," Cee squeaked.

We looked at each other. "The slime ate it," we breathed in unison.

We turned and ran, but we only got two feet before we were forced to a screeching halt.

CHAPTER 17

"Boo!"

The three of us stood paralyzed for two seconds.

Then Cee exploded. "Big Jim," she yelled, "you scared the braids right out of my hair!" She whacked him on the arm.

Big Jim laughed. "What's the matter? Afraid the slime's going to get you?"

My heartbeat slowly wound down to its regular speed. "You wouldn't say that if you knew what just happened to us." I told him the story, and by the end, even Big Jim was glancing around nervously.

"Maybe we should go inside," he suggested, obviously trying not to sound as scared as he looked.

We hurried into Cee's house and up to her room.

Big Jim took the only chair in the room, so the rest

of us had to lounge on Cee's frilly bed or on the floor. He tipped back in the chair.

"Well, girls," he began.

"Girls?" we all repeated, glaring at him.

He grinned and held up his hands as though to fend us off. "Ladies? Women?" He shrugged. "Mutants?"

We nodded.

"Okay, mutants, I've been thinking about our little club and I've decided to volunteer to be the president."

"Boooo," jeered Cee.

"We can vote on that later," Iona said impatiently. "Right now we have to figure out this slime business."

"I think Mr. Verde must be the slime," Cee said. She turned to me. "Remember yesterday when he even turned kind of green?"

Prickles raced up my arms and back. Cee had a point there.

"And what about our powers?" Iona said. "They only came after Big Jim played with Mr. Verde's special yellow liquid that he usually kept under lock and key. Do you think that could have had something to do with it?"

"And he was acting pretty weird after school today," Big Jim added. "Why was he asking us how we felt? Does he know about our mutant powers?"

I looked around at my fellow mutants. "If he does, he probably isn't too happy about it. Maybe that's why we found some slime in this neighborhood. *Our* neighborhood!"

"He's out to slime us!" Cee screeched.

"What are we going to do?" Big Jim asked.

Iona took a deep breath. "We have to solve this ourselves."

Cee nodded. "Righto. But how?"

I swallowed the big lump of fear that clogged my throat. "We have to get rid of the slime ourselves. Before it devours our school and all of us with it."

"Well," said Big Jim, "at least before it slimes *us*. It can have the school."

CHAPTER 18

The next morning, the school bus picked us up the way it did on any weekday, even though it was Saturday. The big Swimathon had finally arrived. Even so, I wasn't as excited as I should have been. Not with the slime problem hanging over my head. Even thoughts of Rick Agent didn't lighten my mood.

The four of us sat on the bus and watched the rain pelt against the front windshield. The big wipers swished back and forth, back and forth.

"How can we get rid of the slime?" Cee finally said, keeping her voice down. "We're just kids."

"And I'm not even an A student," I added glumly.

The rainy, depressing weather really fit our moods.

When we got to school we raced into the building with the other kids, trying to stay as dry as possible, even if we were going to be under water in a few minutes anyway. Despite our efforts, when we got inside, my drenched hair dripped into my eyes, and the bottoms of my pants clung wetly to my legs.

Mr. Verde rushed in at that moment. At first glance we didn't recognize him, he was so bundled up. He wore a wide-brimmed hat pulled low over his ears. He had on a long raincoat and a scarf. His pants were tucked into tall rubber boots, and he even wore gloves and sunglasses.

We tried not to laugh until he had passed us and bustled into the teachers' lounge. Then the laughter sputtered from our lips.

I looked down at my rain-drenched pant legs. "Maybe I should get boots like that," I hooted.

"I'm going to wear my sunglasses next time it rains," Cee said. "I never knew they were called *rainglasses*."

We practically doubled over with laughter.

"What's so funny, *children*?"

We all jerked to attention. Our laughter fizzled away like soda going flat. I hated the way he said "*children*." It made me feel like such a . . . a kid. Hey, I know I'm a kid, but he just made it sound so derogatory. Know what I mean?

Anyway, I had to force my lips into a straight line when I looked at him. "Oh, hi, Mr. Verde."

"Nothing's funny," Iona said.

Mr. Verde narrowed his eyes at us. That's when it hit me that we really shouldn't do anything to annoy

Mr. Verde. After all, if he could slime a car or bleachers, no problem, how easily could he slime us?

He pursed his lips. Then he pivoted and marched away.

I noticed that he looked completely dry, and he still had on his rubber shoes. Not one bit of clothing looked wet. As we slogged down the hall and I wrung out my dripping hair, I thought about adopting his rain gear. It obviously worked.

"We have to do something about the slime," Iona hissed as we walked along.

"Like what?"

"Let's go ask Mrs. Spiegel for help," I suggested.

"Our health teacher?" Big Jim asked.

I nodded.

"You mean, tell her we're mutant kids?" Cee asked.

"No, just tell her we have a slimy thing to get rid of. Maybe she'll have some ideas."

The other three agreed and we hurried to Mrs. Spiegel's classroom, hoping she'd be there, before heading down to the school's indoor pool for the Swimathon. She was in her room wiping her very chalky chalkboards.

"We need to get rid of some slime," I blurted out.

"I'm not quite sure what you're talking about. Exactly what kind of slime is this?"

I said, "You know, like the slime in a drain, only more of it."

"Can't you use one of those drain cleaners?"

We shook our heads.

"Well, I don't know of any stain, slime, or spot that doesn't come out with some cleanser, a lot of water, and a bit of good, hard rubbing." Mrs. Spiegel looked at the cloth in her hand. It was covered with chalk. "Now I have to go rinse this rag so I can clean the rest of my boards. I don't know how they get so dirty." She left the room.

We all seemed to have the same thought at the same time. Cee squirted the boards with water, Big Jim wiped them down at supersonic speed. Iona did the hard-to-reach spots, and I stood invisible in the hall, watching for Mrs. Spiegel.

As soon as I saw her coming, I tapped on the door. No problem. The boards were cleaner than when they were brand-new.

Mrs. Spiegel came in and stood dumbfounded, staring at her chalkboards. "Wha-What happened?"

We all grinned at each other. "Thanks for your help," I said as we left.

"That was fun," Iona giggled as we hurried down to the pool.

"That was the best practical joke I've played on anyone," Big Jim said, beaming with pleasure. "I never knew it could feel so good to be so nice."

Cee rolled her eyes. "Maybe there's hope for you after all." She thumped him on the back.

After I'd changed into my bathing suit, the first person I noticed by the pool was Mr. Verde. He was so noticeable because he stood close to the walls, as far away from the pool as possible. The other teachers all wore shorts or bathing suits. But not Mr. Verde. He was dressed for a winter blizzard.

I shrugged. Maybe Mr. Verde couldn't swim and he was afraid of falling into the water.

Before the races began, there was a short period of free swim.

I waited by the deep end for Cee and Iona and Big Jim. As I waited, I watched all the kids splashing around in the water.

Then I noticed something at the bottom of the deep end. At first I thought it was someone's towel down there. But then I saw it move a little. It wasn't a towel. It was a kid!

CHAPTER 19

Right away I recognized Po Po Sidon's thick dark hair and chubby body.

I waited breathlessly for him to race to the surface, but he just sat on the bottom like a rock.

"Help!" I shouted. "Po Po's drowning!"

I could hardly be heard over all the yelling and shouting. I looked around wildly. Mr. Verde was the closest teacher. I waved frantically to him and pointed into the water. "Po Po's drowning!" I screamed.

Mr. Verde's face grew pale, but he didn't come forward. I couldn't believe it. He was going to let Po Po drown!

I couldn't wait another second. I dove into the water. I should tell you (I'm not bragging, now) that I'm a great swimmer. I already have all my swimming badges, including lifeguarding, even though I'm too young to get the real certificate for it.

Anyway, I dove into the water and swam deep to grab Po Po's lifeless body.

I grabbed his hair, ready to pull him to the surface.

Well, let me tell you, Po Po wasn't exactly dead. In fact, he wasn't anywhere near dead.

As soon as I grabbed him he reared back with surprise. For a second our eyes met. He looked way too alert for someone who had been underwater for the past few minutes, maybe even longer. And he didn't look as if he were about to drown anytime soon, either. In fact, he looked rather annoyed that I still had a clump of his hair in my fist.

Hastily I let go. My lungs were about to burst. Suddenly Po Po grabbed me and dragged me up to the surface just in time for me to gasp for breath.

After I caught my breath, I looked around. No one seemed to have noticed our little adventure. Mr. Verde was nowhere to be seen.

Po Po and I looked at each other.

"You weren't drowning, were you," I said, still trying to catch my breath.

Po Po shook his head. "Not really," he admitted. "I—I learned to hold my breath and dive for long periods of time . . ."

Somehow I knew he was lying. I narrowed my eyes

at him. "There's something fishy about your tale," I said, enjoying my own puns.

Po Po glanced around. When he saw no one was looking at us, he leaned forward and whispered, "Let me tell you a secret. I actually have gills."

"What?"

"I can breathe underwater."

I started laughing.

Po Po looked smug. "I knew you wouldn't believe me," he said, pulling himself out of the water.

I followed him. "Oh, but I do believe you, Po Po."

"You do?" Suddenly he looked worried.

"Sure I do. Now I'll tell you a secret. I can turn invisible."

"You're joking, right?"

"Just like you're joking," I countered, drying off with my towel.

He looked uneasy. He shuffled his feet. I looked down at them and noticed the slight webbing between them. That's when I was sure he was another mutant kid.

"Welcome to the club," I said, grinning.

CHAPTER 20

I saw Cee, Iona, and Big Jim looking for me. I waved them over. Po Po looked kind of worried.

"Let's go over there," I said, motioning toward the corner of the room.

We hustled over there, and when I had their attention I said, "Guess what? Po Po's a mutant, too. He has gills and can breathe underwater!"

Big Jim smacked him on the shoulder. "Welcome to Mutant Kids, Incorporated."

"You mean I'm not the only one with strange new powers?" Po Po said.

Cee shook her head. "I could fill that pool with water in five seconds flat if I had to."

"And I could stand in the deep end without getting my hair wet," Iona said.

Big Jim grinned. "And I could swim in circles so fast I'd cause a whirlpool."

Po Po looked around. "Hey, where's JP?"

"Right here," I said, reappearing.

Po Po's eyes popped out of his head so much he looked like one of those puffer fish.

"How did you discover your new talent?" Iona asked.

Po Po blushed. "Goofing around in the bathtub."

Big Jim nodded. "Right after the science experiment I did in Verde's class, right?"

Po Po nodded. "That night, as a matter of fact."

"This means there must be other mutants in that class," Cee said.

We all looked around at all the kids yelling and diving and swimming.

"I wonder what their powers are," I said.

"I'll tell you what mine is," said a voice.

We looked around, but only the five of us were standing in the corner.

"I'm over here," the voice said.

We turned toward the voice—toward the wall.

For a moment I thought there must be another invisible kid like me, but then a really strange thing happened.

A hand popped out of the wall!

CHAPTER 21

I would have recognized that hand anywhere. It belonged to Rick Agent! But where was the rest of him?

Next, his head came out of the wall. He looked around to make sure no one was watching him besides us; then the rest of his body popped out.

Even though we were pretty cool about these strange new powers we all had, seeing Rick walk through the wall was pretty awesome.

Before we could say anything, Rick held up his hand. "I know all about you mutants," he said. "I've heard you talking."

"Why didn't you tell us about your power before?" Iona asked. "Instead of sneaking around on us."

"I wasn't sneaking," Rick protested. "Every time I was going to show myself to you, you all left or something happened so I couldn't. I wasn't spying."

"I'm sure you weren't," I said quickly, coming to his defense. The smile he gave me was worth it. "Anyway, we know about it now. Now there are six of us mutants."

I was about to add more about our club when Sue Duffy walked by. We all stared at her as if she were from outer space or something. No, she didn't have green skin or antennae coming out of her head or anything, but she was cracking up like crazy. In fact, she was laughing so hard, tears were flowing out her eyes like Niagara Falls.

"What's so funny, Space-out?" Big Jim called.

Sue looked over at us through her tears. She came over, trying to control her laughter, but every once in a while a big giggle escaped.

She shook her head, trying to talk. "It's just so funny," she gasped.

"What is?" Cee demanded.

"Mr. Strikes's underwear!" Loud laughter followed these words.

The rest of us looked at each other and shrugged.

"What about his underwear?" Rick asked.

"They have Batman all over them!" Howls of laughter pierced the air as Sue lost all control.

I started to giggle, imagining our stern Mr. Strikes in Batman underwear. My fellow mutants seemed to find it amusing also. Pretty soon we were all laughing.

When we finally caught our breaths, I asked, "How do you know he's wearing Batman underwear, anyway?"

"I have X-ray vision." As soon as the words were out, Sue clapped her hand across her mouth. "Ooops," she said. "I wasn't going to tell anyone."

"You mean you really can see through stuff?" Big Jim asked. He shifted uncomfortably. "Like through walls and doors and *clothes*?"

"Don't worry," Sue said, wiping away her laughter tears. "There's nothing under your clothes I want to see, especially not that pink underwear you're wearing."

Rick looked at Big Jim. "Pink?"

Big Jim blushed. He looked as if he wanted to push Sue into the pool. "They used to be white," he mumbled. "Mom didn't tell me to separate the whites from the colors when I washed them until it was too late."

We all laughed, but not too hard because it was clear Big Jim was totally embarrassed. (I have to admit, it was nice to have *him* be the embarrassed one for a change.)

Big Jim was glad to change the subject and explain to Sue about our mutant powers. Pretty soon we had all made a pledge to be loyal members of Mutant Kids, Inc., and not to tell anyone else about our powers, unless, of course, we found more mutants like us.

With that settled, I said, "Let's go swimming now. I want to warm up for the races."

We had a great time that morning. We splashed and swam. Our relay team won (thanks to Big Jim), and Rick even hugged me! I thought I would die. Finally it was time for the boxed sandwiches the cafeteria ladies had prepared for us the day before.

Quickly we dried off and changed. Then we met next to the gym doors.

"Let's go eat," Big Jim said, rubbing a big hand over his big belly.

Everyone agreed, and we had just started walking when Mr. Strikes shouted, "JP, stop right there!"

CHAPTER 22

We all turned toward Mr. Strikes.

"Hello, kids," he said.

We all nodded, staring at the floor. I think we were afraid we'd burst into laughter if we looked at him, knowing he was wearing Batman underwear.

"JP," he said, "have you seen Mr. Verde?"

"No, I haven't seen him lately. I saw him standing over there a while ago," I added, pointing to where he had been standing when he wouldn't save Po Po.

Mr. Strikes frowned. "If you see him, tell him I'm looking for him." He turned to go, and I shrugged at my friends. Suddenly he turned around again. "Oh, I almost forgot. Your mom called and your little brother's craft class was canceled. You have to go pick him up at his school."

"But what about the rest of the Swimathon?" I wailed.

Mr. Strikes wrinkled his forehead. "I suppose you can bring him back here for the rest of the day. But he can't go swimming."

"No problem," I said. "He doesn't know how to swim, anyway."

"That's settled then," Mr. Strikes said as he bustled off. "Remember," he called over his shoulder. "If you see Mr. Verde . . ."

"Maybe he knows he's the slime," Cee whispered.

"What slime?" Sue asked.

Quickly we filled in our latest mutant clubmates on the slime and our theory about Mr. Verde.

"Why don't we try to find him?" Rick suggested.

Sue looked around the room. "I don't see him." Then she stopped. "Wait, there he is, in the gym storage room."

"How can you—" Po Po began. "Oh yeah," he said with a grin. "X-ray eyes."

"Come on, let's go," Rick said.

We hurried out of the pool room and down the long corridor by the double gyms. When we rounded the far corner we put fingers to our lips to remind ourselves to be quiet. Spying on Mr. Verde was one thing, but having him *see us* spying was another.

The big metal door of the supply room was open.

Carefully we tiptoed forward. Cee was in the lead, with me right behind her. I don't know who was right behind me, but whoever it was kept stepping on my heels. I would've turned around and yelled at her or him, but I didn't want to attract Mr. Verde's attention.

As we neared the door we fanned out so we could peer around the sides of the door frame without, we hoped, being seen.

Sue crouched next to me. We saw Mr. Verde fumbling around in the bags of balls. Every once in a while he picked up a ball and sniffed it the way my Mom does the melons at the store. Then he tossed it aside. Pretty soon there were basketballs and soccer balls bouncing all over the crowded room.

"What's he doing?" I whispered to anyone within hearing distance.

Sue shrugged and whispered back, "Maybe he's getting a ball for the pool games or something."

"Then why is he smelling them?"

Sue put her hand over her mouth to stop a giggle from escaping. I have no idea what she thought was so funny.

"Should I tell him Mr. Strikes is looking for him?" I asked, being sure to keep my voice to the softest whisper possible.

"Go ahead," said Big Jim, leaning closer to my ear. "We'll wait out here for you."

"Gee, thanks," I said. It's hard to sound sarcastic when you're whispering, but Big Jim got the message. He grinned.

Just as I was about to step forward, Sue put her hand on my arm. "Wait!"

My heart jumped at the sudden warning. "What?"

She put a finger to her lips. "There's something really strange about Mr. Verde."

"No kidding," said Iona. "What do you think we were telling you before about the slime?"

"Well, I didn't really believe that," Sue answered back. "But there is definitely something weird about him."

"What is it?" Rick asked.

Sue looked at us with wide eyes. "Mr. Verde doesn't have any bones."

CHAPTER 23

We all turned to stare at our science teacher, who was still sniffing balls.

"No bones?" Po Po squeaked. "How is that possible?"

"I don't know," said Sue, "but when I look at any of you, I can clearly see your skeleton. Mr. Verde is just a blob."

"I knew it," Cee whispered, her voice getting a little too loud for my comfort. "It's 'cause he's the slime."

"I still think I should tell him Mr. Strikes is looking for him," I said. "We don't want him to think we're suspicious of him."

"I'm not sure it's safe," Rick whispered in my ear. "Maybe I should tell him."

I glowed with pleasure. Rick wanted to take my place so I wouldn't get slimed. Kind of romantic, don't you think? Okay, so it's not a dozen red roses, but what kid wants flowers?

"That's okay," I heard myself saying. "I'm not scared." What, was I crazy?

Once again I was about to step forward, half hoping someone would stop me, when I froze in my tracks. I heard everyone behind me gasp for breath. It's a wonder Mr. Verde didn't hear all of us freaking out.

But of course he didn't hear us, he was too busy turning into *the slime*!

Right before our eyes his skeletonless body mutated into a shapeless, green, gurgling mass. The slime quivered and jiggled right there in front of us like a giant blob of melting lime Jello-O.

Someone grabbed my arm and squeezed tight. I grabbed someone else's arm. I could feel the fear racing through us, as though we were linked by a big electrical current.

So far the slime hadn't noticed us. It slurped its body over one of the many gym balls. Then, with a loud sucking sound, it moved on to the next one.

The slime was eating—if you can call it that—the balls!

"Grossssss," Cee hissed behind me. "A rubber snack."

"Shhh," I warned her without turning around. The last thing we wanted to do was get the slime's attention.

Now you're probably thinking that we should have been miles away from there by then. I mean, who in their right mind would hang around when their science teacher had turned into a hungry, slimy monster? Maybe our new mutant powers made us stupid or something. I don't know. Or maybe it was the fear. Whatever the reason, we were glued to that doorway, watching in horrified fascination as the slime devoured all the balls in the storage room.

Then the most disgusting thing happened. The slime let out a big, rubbery burp.

Totally gross!

My brother, Brian, has occasional lapses in his manners when he burps as long and loud as he can. But even he would have been impressed with this one.

Big Jim was impressed too.

"Awesome," he said under his breath.

I glanced at Cee and we rolled our eyes. Knowing our luck, from now on Big Jim would try to outburp the slime.

Just then Iona whispered, "We have to do something about the slime."

"Like what?" Po Po asked. "He's a lot slimier and hungrier than we are."

"But we can't just let him get away," Rick said softly. "That thing will slime the whole school next, and then the town!"

Big Jim nodded. "I don't mind the school part, but

it would rot not to have a town anymore. Where would we live?"

"You probably wouldn't have to worry about that," Sue said gloomily. "He'll probably slime all the people for dessert."

Big Jim turned kind of pale. "Oh. I never looked at it like that."

"Well look at *that*!" Cee squealed, pointing a shaky finger into the storage room.

CHAPTER 24

As we had been talking, our attention had wandered away from the slime, which was gurgling and feeling around for more rubber food.

But now we all stared as the slime slowly shaped back into Mr. Verde.

As a "human" once again, Mr. Verde looked around the storage room. He hadn't slimed any of the bats or rackets, just the balls. Off in one corner he spotted a baseball he'd missed. He picked it up. I thought he was going to toss it aside when his head turned back into the slime and he shoved the baseball into the jiggling mass. The ball was swallowed up in the green slime, and Mr. Verde's head reshaped into the balding form we knew so well.

Iona chose that inappropriate time to gasp. I mean,

there had been plenty of times earlier that had deserved a gasp, or she could have saved it till we were safely away. But no, she had to gasp at that moment. Out loud. And I mean *loud*.

Mr. Verde spun around. We were so surprised we all kind of fell into the doorway and huddled and sprawled and squatted there like a bunch of chickens headed for the slaughterhouse.

"Uh, hi, Mr. Verde," I managed to squeak out.

"How long have you kids been there?" he demanded.

"Long enough," blurted out big-mouthed Big Jim. "We saw it all."

"Shut up!" Sue cried. "Are you trying to get us slimed?"

Then, before we knew it, Mr. Verde was no longer merely a science teacher with really bad taste in clothes. He was the slime!

"Run!" I shouted.

Easier shouted than done. About three people had to scramble to their feet before I could haul myself up to a standing position and get out of there.

Big Jim ran off, no problem. You would have thought he'd take at least one of us with him. But nooooo.

"This way," Sue called, in the lead.

We hurled ourselves down the hallway.

"Shouldn't we head back to the pool and cafeteria and other people?" I shouted as we ran.

"Should have," Sue called back. "But I went the wrong way."

Then I remembered Sue hadn't been at the school last year. She had no idea where she was going. So why was she leading the way?

"Take the next right," I shouted ahead.

Either Sue didn't hear me or she ignored me. You guessed it, she kept going straight.

"Split up," Cee gasped next to me. "He can't chase us all."

I nodded and took off to the right. I looked behind me and saw that Po Po was desperately trying to keep up. He only had powers under water, so running wasn't any easier for him than it had been. And it wasn't any easier for me either, except that I'm in pretty great shape anyway.

Just then Rick appeared half in and half out of the wall up ahead. "Is the slime coming?" he asked.

"How'd you get so far ahead of us?" I demanded as I ran by him.

He grinned. "I just ran through the classrooms. Oh, and the walls." Then he slipped out of sight.

I looked behind me again. "Come on, Po Po. I think we've lost him. But let's just go around the corner to be sure."

Poor Po Po was barely limping along. Good thing the slime hadn't followed us or Po Po definitely would have been the first mutant to be slimed.

When we rounded the corner, we didn't see any slime or any other mutants either.

"You stay here, Po Po. I'm going to make sure everyone's okay."

For a minute Po Po couldn't say anything; he was trying to catch his breath. I even caught a glimpse of his gills flapping behind his ears.

"Are . . . you . . . sure . . . it's . . . safe?" he finally gasped.

"No," I said curtly. I mean, come on, we knew the slime was totally *un*safe. Not exactly the brightest question, I thought, but then again, Po Po's brain was obviously starving for oxygen. "But I'll be okay like this."

I wished myself invisible. I could tell by Po Po's widened eyes that it had worked.

"Don't go anywhere," I said. "I'll try to bring everyone back here."

Po Po looked around uneasily, but he nodded.

I waved, realizing at the last moment it wouldn't do any good. Then I took off at a fast jog to look for my mutant friends.

CHAPTER 25

As I ran, I was glad that I had on sneakers because they made little to no noise on the linoleum floors of the hallways.

In fact, Cee didn't even hear me coming until I said, "Boo!" right next to her.

I made myself visible and she glared at me as if she wanted to melt me down into a pile of goo, kind of like the slime.

"Don't ever do that to me again!"

I smiled at her. "Sorry." I knew she couldn't stay mad at me for long. "Where's the slime?" I asked.

"I lost it. I took a left when you took a right, and the slime actually came after me for a few doors. But suddenly it stopped and turned around. I haven't seen it since."

"Why did it stop chasing you?"

Cee shrugged. "Beats me. I didn't stop it to ask why."

"What about the others? I left Po Po safe over by Mrs. Cocco's cooking classroom."

Cee shrugged again. "Rick popped out of a wall, but then he disappeared again. Big Jim is long gone. Sue went straight when we turned, and I think Iona followed her."

"We'd better find them," I said.

We started walking quickly but cautiously back down the corridor.

"Hey!" I exclaimed, looking down. "Have you been leaking? The floor's all wet."

Cee nodded sheepishly. "I guess I leak a little when I get nervous." She held up her pinkie, which was leaking more than just a little.

"Oh well," I said. "We'll worry about your faucet fingers later. Right now we have to make sure all our mutant club members are safe."

We turned and followed the direction we thought Sue and Iona must have taken. It led right to the big double doors of the auditorium.

Slowly and carefully, and hoping the hinges wouldn't squeak, we pushed open the heavy door. The auditorium was dark except for a faint light up onstage.

I motioned to Cee to come on.

The floor was carpeted, and every once in a while I imagined I could feel a slimy, slippery goo under my sneakers. But I didn't dare stop to look. Too much was at stake. First we had to find our friends.

When we got to the stage we looked around in the dim light. I didn't see anything. It was hard to imagine the stage crowded with kids for the racetrack scene in *My Fair Lady* when all I could picture in my mind was a gurgling green glop of goo.

"Iona?" I called softly. "Sue?"

"I'm up here," came a shivering voice.

"Sue?"

"No, it's Iona," she said. Suddenly a long thin body stretched down from the immense curtain rod hanging across the stage.

She looked around warily before shrinking down to her own size, checking the length of her jeans as she did so.

"He chased us in here," Iona explained. She pointed to a side door. "I escaped up there, but Sue had no choice but to run through the backstage doors. The slime stopped for a moment and gurgled at me, but then it went on after Sue."

"Sheesh!" exclaimed Cee. "I hope she got away."

"There's only one way to find out," I said. "Let's go."

Now we ran across the stage and banged through the back doors.

At that moment I happened to glance at my wrist. "Oh no!" I cried.

CHAPTER 26

"What's wrong?" asked Cee, bumping into me when I stopped dead in my tracks.

"I have to meet Brian at Sieffert Elementary. I'm already late."

"But what about the slime?" Iona wailed.

"You guys will have to go on and find everyone. Don't forget to get Po Po. He's waiting for you in front of Mrs. Cocco's room." I dashed toward the closest exit. "I'll get Brian and meet you back here by the pool. We should all be safe there."

"Righto," Cee called after me as I slammed out of the building.

Outside, the sun had come out. It was hot. Most of the earlier rain had dried up except for a few big puddles here and there. Pretty nice weather for September.

As I ran, I tried not to think about the danger my mutant friends were in. I just hoped they'd be able to lure the slime back to the gym pool, where—I hoped—they'd be safe. Surely the slime wouldn't attempt to slime all the kids and even Mr. Strikes?

Glancing at my watch, I saw I was already pretty late. I knew it would be impossible to convince Brian to keep his mouth shut about me being late. He'd blab to Mom as soon as we got home. Then Mom would kill me.

If the slime didn't get me first.

Yuck. I shook that thought away.

I finally rounded the last corner fifteen minutes late and zoomed toward Brian's elementary school. All the cars in the parking lot were gone. My heart thudded in my chest, and not because I was running so fast.

What if someone had kidnapped Brian? Then my Mom would *really* kill me. Besides, even though he was a brat, I'd still miss him.

Where was he?

I ran around to the back of the school and sighed with relief. Brian buzzed around the playscape. A teacher had stayed with him.

As I ran closer, the teacher called to Brian and my brother skipped over to him.

The teacher grabbed him.

I almost fainted right in my tracks. That wasn't Brian's teacher—it was Mr. Verde!

CHAPTER 27

Brian kicked and waved his arms around like a windmill. "Let me go, you creep," he yelled. "I'll tell my mommy on you!"

"Let him go," I screamed, running closer.

I was about to tackle Mr. Verde and throw him to the ground when he started to change. His skin melted into green globs until he was a big pile of slime, blubbering in front of me. And he still held on to Brian.

Brian's eyes bulged out of their sockets with fear. I almost felt sorry for him.

Almost.

My mind raced frantically. How would I save my brother?

"Hey, slime," I shouted. "Come and get me!" I ran

a few steps; then I stopped. Sure enough, the slime slid toward me.

I wished myself invisible. Poor Brian. I thought he was going to pass out when I disappeared.

"Come on, slime," I taunted. "What's the matter? Can't you see me?"

I popped into visibility again and the slime headed toward me. I let it get a lot closer; then I vanished.

I could tell the slime was confused. I knew if I could keep this up, it would forget to slime Brian, even though it still held my brother under one slimy arm. I would have to lure it back to school and hope that my mutant friends had thought of a way to vanquish the slime once and for all.

At least I knew they hadn't been slimed because the slime was out here chasing me.

I kept teasing and yelling at the slime, drawing him closer and closer to my school. Mostly he just slithered along, green and disgusting, but every once in a while he turned into Mr. Verde, rubber boots and all.

Only a few cars passed us on the quiet streets. A couple of them slowed down, and the drivers stared at us. But then they zoomed off. I can just imagine what they told their families that night. They probably thought the slime was an early Halloween costume or something.

Finally I rounded the last corner. I never thought I'd be so happy to see the front of my school. I charged up the steps and pushed open the massive front door. The slime slid up behind me, still hanging on to my brother.

Brian hung like a limp rag doll under the slime's arm. Well, it wasn't really an arm. It was more like a big, gooey glob that held Brian up against the slime. I hoped Brian had passed out so he wouldn't remember any of this.

I ran down the hall toward the gym area, but when I came to a T in the hall I suddenly panicked. Don't ask me why. After all, this was my second year at Kiernan Middle School. It wasn't as if I didn't know where I was going. But at that moment that's exactly what happened. I guess it was because I had this slimy green fungus following me. Which way to the gym? To the pool? To safety?

The slobbering, sucking sound of the slime got closer and closer. I turned my head back and forth, back and forth.

Which way?

My nerves screamed with fear.

I had to do something. Fast!

I started to the left.

No!

That was the wrong way!

I pivoted and dashed back the other way.

The slime shot out a glob, trying to grab me.

I felt like a fly, dodging a frog's tongue. I barely made it.

I raced down the hall. Had I gone the right way?

CHAPTER 28

Yes!

Ahead of me I saw the bright blue gym doors. I knew once I found my mutant friends and we were surrounded by the rest of the school, including the principal, everything would be okay. Mr. Verde would have no choice but to give me my brother back. And we'd all live happily ever after, right?

Not!

I couldn't believe it. The gym doors were locked!

I pounded on them. I yanked on them. Nothing!

I was trapped.

Ssshhhhlllllluuuurrrrrrp!

Ugh. Just the noises it made caused my stomach to turn.

The slime slid forward.

In a panic, I wished myself invisible. At least I had my mutant power. Then, taking a deep breath, I charged by the slime. Even though he couldn't see me, he seemed to sense me as I whizzed by. He shot out a glob of goo, but too late.

I couldn't believe my luck. I had escaped!

I have to admit I was tempted to just stay invisible and run all the way home and hide under my bed. Forget Brian! But I didn't.

Once I was past the danger zone, I made myself visible again.

"Here I am, slimebag," I taunted.

The slime slithered around and chased after me.

There was no hope of going back to the gym, so I raced upstairs and eventually ended up in Mr. Verde's science room.

Gasping for breath, I hid behind his big table. I peeked over the top. Any second I expected the slime to suck its way into the classroom. Instead, Mr. Verde stepped in, still lugging Brian under one arm. He slammed the door shut behind him.

"I know you're here, Ms. Price," he said. He shook Brian. "Don't you want your brother back?"

Warily I stood up, wondering what had happened to my mutant friends. "Not really," I said, wishing my voice didn't quiver so much. "He's a brat. You can have him."

Mr. Verde's eyebrows shot up over his forehead. "But he's your brother," he protested.

"I know, but he's a pest. And he always tattles on me."

Brian no longer hung limply under Mr. Verde's arm. He wiggled and twisted, turning this way and that, trying to spot me. "I'm going to tell Mommy on you," he said. "I'm going to tell her you didn't want me."

"See?" I said.

Mr. Verde frowned. He dropped Brian.

I winced. That looked a little painful.

Brian crawled to the nearest table.

"All I really want is you and your busybody friends, anyway." Mr. Verde grinned an evil green grin. "With you gone, no one will know anything about me."

I gasped.

No doubt Mr. Verde thought it had something to do with what he'd said, but really it was because I saw Rick come through the wall behind Mr. Verde. He held his finger to his lips.

Finally, I thought. Help is on the way!

More to keep him busy than because I really wanted to know, I started asking Mr. Verde questions.

"Who are you?"

He shrugged as though he didn't think it would matter how many secrets he told me because I'd be slime soup pretty soon. "My name is Slllrmp. We are having a severe food shortage on our planet. I'm here to find out if you have an adequate food supply here for us."

Just the way he looked at me and licked his lips made me nervous. "Uh, do we?"

He just laughed.

"Do all of you look like—like green slime?" I couldn't help asking.

He nodded. "I can look human, but only with the help of my yellow potion."

"You mean the one Big Jim used—" I clapped my hand over my mouth.

"Aha, so he was the culprit," Mr. Verde spat out. "It'll be a pleasure seeing him again. You see, when he used up my potion, I was unable to control my human form for long. Now it's very difficult for me to keep my human form, so I had to speed up the search for an alternate food source before returning to my planet."

"So you're going back to your planet?" I asked hopefully.

"After I get rid of you nosy kids."

"Why do you have to get rid of us if you're going back to your own planet?"

"Because I'll be coming back to Earth with my friends and family. We're *all* hungry, remember? And

I don't want any panicky humans ruining my plans to return."

I think that was the closest I've ever come to fainting.

Just then the door banged open. Mr. Verde swung around, and I almost cheered for joy.

CHAPTER 29

Never had a bunch of mutants looked so good. They burst through the door. Po Po was last, and he quickly shut the door behind them.

"We've got you now, slimeball!" Big Jim shouted.

Mr. Verde simply crossed his arms and laughed. "Oh, really? And how might you do that? You're only kids, after all."

"Make that *mutant* kids," Sue said, glaring at him with her X-ray eyes.

"We'll find a way to slime the slime," Cee said, sounding braver than she looked. I noticed her pinkie was on steady leak mode.

Suddenly Mr. Verde yelled so loudly I thought I'd be hard of hearing for weeks afterward. "You can't destroy me! I won't let you. I'll get you first!"

He lunged toward me. I dodged out of the way and

crashed into Rick by accident. We both fell to the floor. Before we could untangle ourselves, Mr. Verde was towering over us. His skin began to change color. Soon he was a mutated mass of slime.

"Help!" I yelled. "Someone do something!"

Cee lifted her fingers and pointed them at the slime as though she were going to cast a spell.

Suddenly water gushed out from the tips of her fingers as if she'd turned on ten faucets full blast.

The slime quivered and gurgled. It backed away.

Cee kept the water coming on strong. It came out so fast, the room began to flood. Rick and I scrambled to our feet. Soon the water rose to my knees. It crept higher and higher with each passing second.

The slime flailed around as though it was trying to swim.

But it was no use.

It was melting!

"Help!" Brian cried.

I jerked around. The water was now up to my waist. My brother stood off to the side and wildly flung his arms around. The water rose to his shoulders.

"Help!" he cried. "I can't swim!"

CHAPTER 30

I sloshed through the water and grabbed Brian under the arms. He clung to me like a scared monkey.

The water kept rising. Now there was no sign of the slime, but the water glowed green. Big bubbles rose from the center of the room where the slime had been.

Cee kept the waterfalls flowing from her fingers. Iona stretched taller as the water rose. I didn't see Po Po anywhere, but I didn't worry about him in all this water. He was probably having a great time swimming between the table legs.

I pushed my way through the flood to the door. I turned the knob. Not the brightest thing to do, I must admit.

The door burst open and the water gushed out of the room, tumbling all of us along with it.

All I remember are arms and legs and the corners of a few science manuals that were washed down the hall with us.

By the time we hit the end of the hall, the oomph had gone out of the flood. Brian, Sue, Big Jim, and I lay there in a clump, staring at each other. Nearby, Po Po was flopping around in the water like a fish. Rick peered out at us from the wall. When he saw that we were okay, he grinned.

Water kept gushing by.

"Where are Cee and Iona?" I asked in alarm, but just then Iona walked out of the classroom. Her clothes were perfectly dry.

"Only my stretchable ankles got wet," she explained when she saw me staring at her.

I pushed some sopping wet hair out of my eyes. "This was the most exciting Swimathon I've ever been to!"

Everyone laughed.

Finally Cee came into the hallway.

"Is he gone?" Rick asked.

Cee grinned and nodded. "Not a slimy sign of him anywhere," she announced.

'How did you know he would melt like that?" Sue asked.

Cee grinned. "It just kind of all fit together at the last minute. He was always afraid of water, like when he came in from the rain, and he wouldn't stand too

109

close to the pool, and he stopped chasing me earlier when I started leaking water. And how quickly it disappeared off that doorknob when I squirted it. And I remember what Mrs. Spiegel said about how water and a good scrubbing will get rid of almost any slime."

"She was right!" I said, getting to my feet and trying to wring some of the water out of my clothes.

"It's a good thing you have water fingers for a mutant power," Po Po said.

"Yeah," Big Jim said. "Or we'd all be slimed for sure."

Cee beamed. "You're right. I guess my mutant power is good for something after all!"

We all cheered.

"I'm going to tell Mommy you got me all wet," Brian said.

I rolled my eyes and tousled his wet hair. "At least my dear little brother wasn't slimed," I said with a snort.

*　*　*

Well, that's pretty much how our adventure with the slime ended. We found Mr. Strikes and told him there must have been a leaky water pipe in Mr. Verde's room.

For a couple of days we had a substitute science

teacher, and then they hired Ms. Rose. She's the best! She has good taste in clothes, and she even calls me JP.

As for our club, we meet every Tuesday night. That's when we plan our good-deed practical jokes. We decided to use our powers only for good things. I know that sounds kind of corny, but hey, we're basically good kids. Even Big Jim, though he can still be a pain.

And if you're ever traveling through the United States and you hear of a town where weird things happen, it's a good chance it's our town. But you'll never know for sure because, remember, I've changed all our names to protect the members of Mutant Kids, Inc.

LAURA E. WILLIAMS taught middle-school and high-school English for eight years. Now she spends her day chasing and kissing her kids, figuring out ways not to clean her house, and writing books in her spare time. She claims she met some honest-to-goodness mutant kids when she was teaching. Ms. Williams lives in Avon Lake, Ohio.